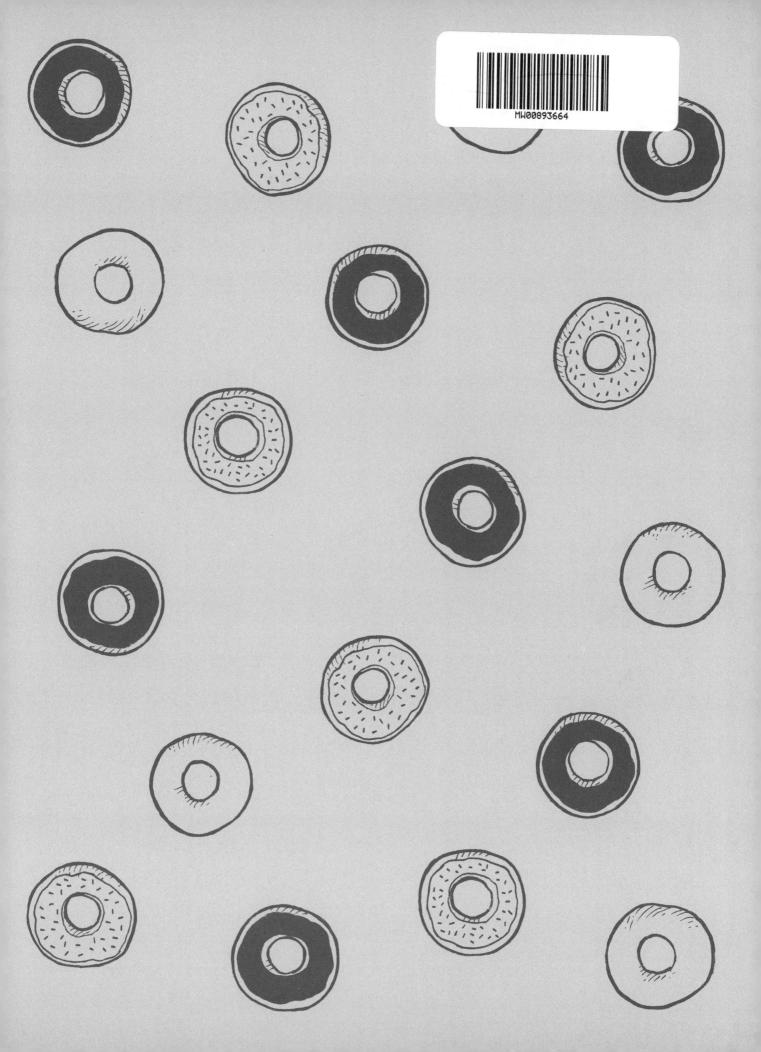

PUG & DOUG

story and pictures by
STEVE BREEN

Dial Books for Young Readers
an imprint of Penguin Group (USA) Inc.

For Cate

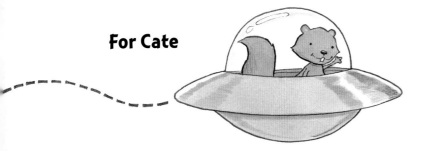

DIAL BOOKS FOR YOUNG READERS
A division of Penguin Young Readers Group
Published by The Penguin Group
Penguin Group (USA) Inc., 375 Hudson Street, New York, NY 10014, U.S.A.
Penguin Group (Canada), 90 Eglinton Avenue East, Suite 700, Toronto, Ontario, Canada M4P 2Y3 (a division of Pearson Penguin Canada Inc.)
Penguin Books Ltd, 80 Strand, London WC2R 0RL, England
Penguin Ireland, 25 St. Stephen's Green, Dublin 2, Ireland (a division of Penguin Books Ltd)
Penguin Group (Australia), 250 Camberwell Road, Camberwell, Victoria 3124, Australia (a division of Pearson Australia Group Pty Ltd)
Penguin Books India Pvt Ltd, 11 Community Centre, Panchsheel Park, New Delhi - 110 017, India
Penguin Group (NZ), 67 Apollo Drive, Rosedale, Auckland 0632, New Zealand (a division of Pearson New Zealand Ltd)
Penguin Books (South Africa) (Pty) Ltd, 24 Sturdee Avenue, Rosebank, Johannesburg 2196, South Africa
Penguin Books Ltd, Registered Offices: 80 Strand, London WC2R 0RL, England

Designed by Lily Malcom
Text set in Montara
Manufactured in China on acid-free paper

10 9 8 7 6 5 4 3 2 1

Library of Congress Cataloging-in-Publication Data
Breen, Steve.
 Pug & Doug / story and pictures by Steve Breen.
   p. cm.
 Summary: Pug and Doug are best friends, even when their differences lead to a misunderstanding.
 ISBN 978-0-8037-3521-7 (hardcover)
 [1. Best friends—Fiction. 2. Friendship—Fiction. 3. Dogs—Fiction.] I. Title. II. Title: Pug and Doug.
 PZ7.B748228Pug 2013
 [E]—dc23   2012014704

The illustrations for this book were created using watercolor and acrylic paint, colored pencil, and Photoshop.

Pug and Doug lived next door to each other in the little town of Squirrel Hill. They were always hanging out doing stuff together, because that's what best friends do.

They watched
movies together,

they ate snacks together,

and they listened to polka music together.

Pug and Doug had tons in common too.

For instance, they both enjoyed bird-watching

. . . and they were both afraid of:

vampires

mummies

Chinese crested shorthairs.

They were such good friends that Pug and Doug
even had a secret pawshake.

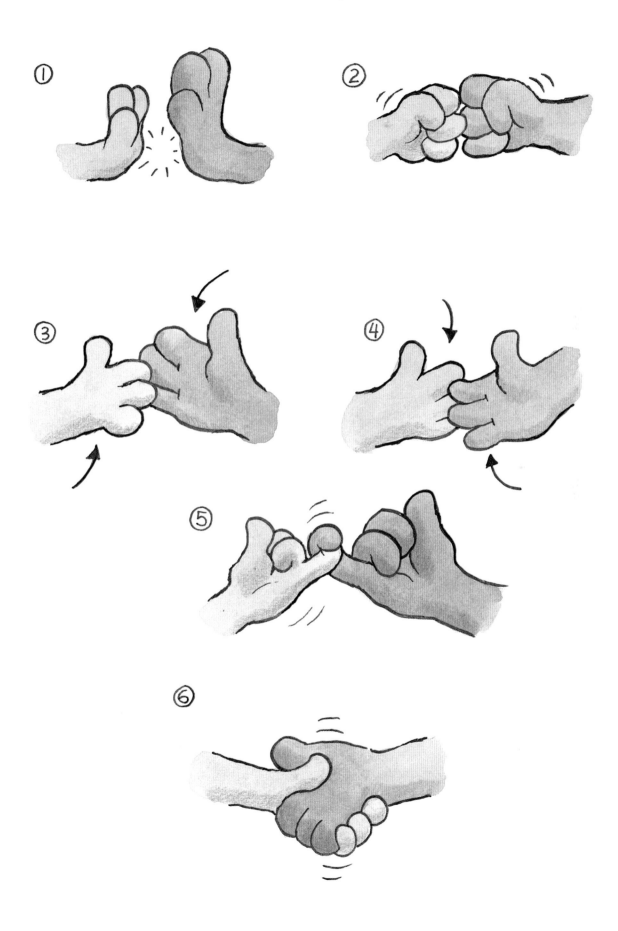

Despite all this, Pug and Doug were pretty different.

Doug was artistic.

Pug not so much.

Not surprisingly, Doug had more of an imagination than Pug.

Sometimes Doug could annoy Pug a little,

sometimes a lot.

And Doug thought that sometimes Pug could be a real stick-in-the-mud.

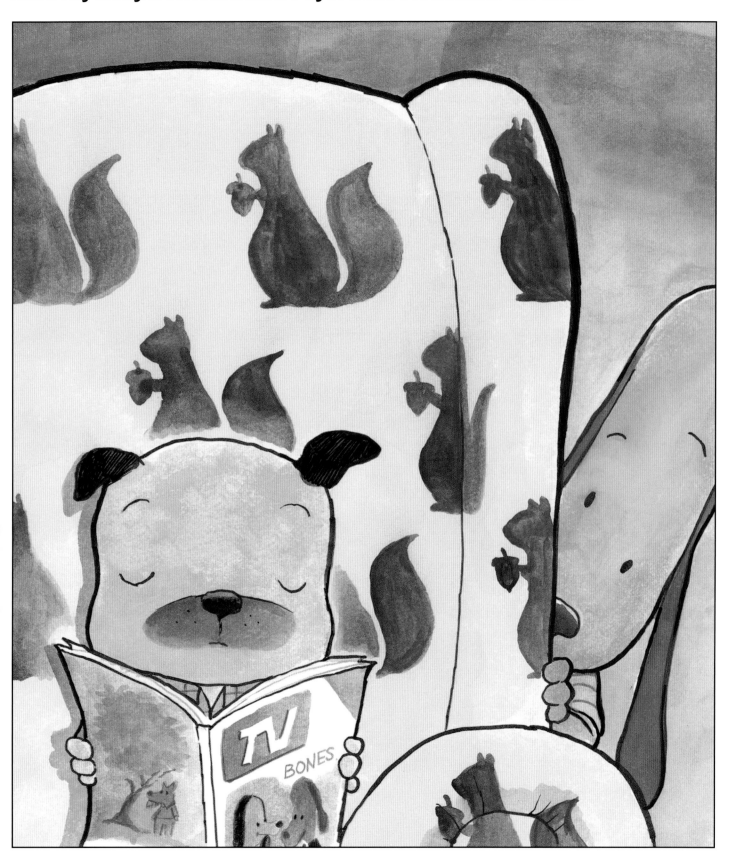

When Pug got in one of his moods, Doug would
leave him alone and go to his own house.

One day, Doug walked past Pug's trash can at the curb and noticed that inside was a picture of the two of them at last year's UFO convention.

When Doug went to ask why Pug had thrown the photo away, Pug came rushing out of the house.

"Can't talk now, Doug . . . I, uh . . . gotta run downtown to pick up a friend."

Doug felt ignored.

That night, when Doug went over to see if Pug wanted to watch a movie, he heard that Pug already had company.

Nobody answered the door, so Doug peeked in the window. He happened to look down at Pug's open diary. "I'm really sick of old Doug," it read.

Doug was heartbroken.
"Pug is tired of me," he said.

The next day was Doug's birthday. Pug excitedly walked over to Doug's house to give his pal a gift: a pet parrot named Buddy.

Nobody was home when Pug rang the bell. Then he noticed a note addressed "To Pug" taped to the door.

Pug was surprised. "Why does
Doug think I'm sick of him?
I have to find him!"

Pug and Buddy searched the whole town for Doug,
but couldn't find him anywhere.

Pug went home to feed Buddy. "Good gravy! My open diary was right by the window . . . Doug must have seen it. I bet this is why he thinks I'm sick of him."

Pug meant to write "I'M REALLY SICK OF OLD DOUGHNUTS," but he got distracted by a squirrel outside and didn't finish the sentence.

"Where could Doug be?"

Pug did his best thinking outside, so he lay on a hill
and stared at the sky. As he watched the clouds drift
past, he noticed that one looked like a UFO.

"That's it! I know where Doug is!"

Pug and Buddy quickly went to the bus station and caught the westbound 225.

There was one seat left.

When the bus stopped at the convention center, Pug and Buddy hopped off and raced toward the building.

Once inside, Pug borrowed a jetpack from a conventioneer.

He flew over the crowd in circles until he finally located Doug.

"What are you doing here?" Doug asked.
"I came here to find you because I am not sick of you! What
you read in my diary was not the whole story," said Pug,
and he explained the misunderstanding.

"But you threw away the souvenir photo we took here last year," said Doug.

"What? I didn't mean to. I was cleaning out my den and I must have put it in the trash by mistake," said Pug.

"But then you ignored me to pick up a friend downtown."

"I was getting your *birthday present!* Doug, meet Buddy."
Doug was a little embarrassed and petted Buddy on the head.
"Thanks, Pug. I'm sorry I let my imagination get away from me."
"No worries, amigo," replied Pug. The old pals then did their
secret pawshake.

Pug and Doug left the convention and headed home. They agreed that
a good way to avoid hurt feelings in the future was to talk things over.
Because that's what best friends do.

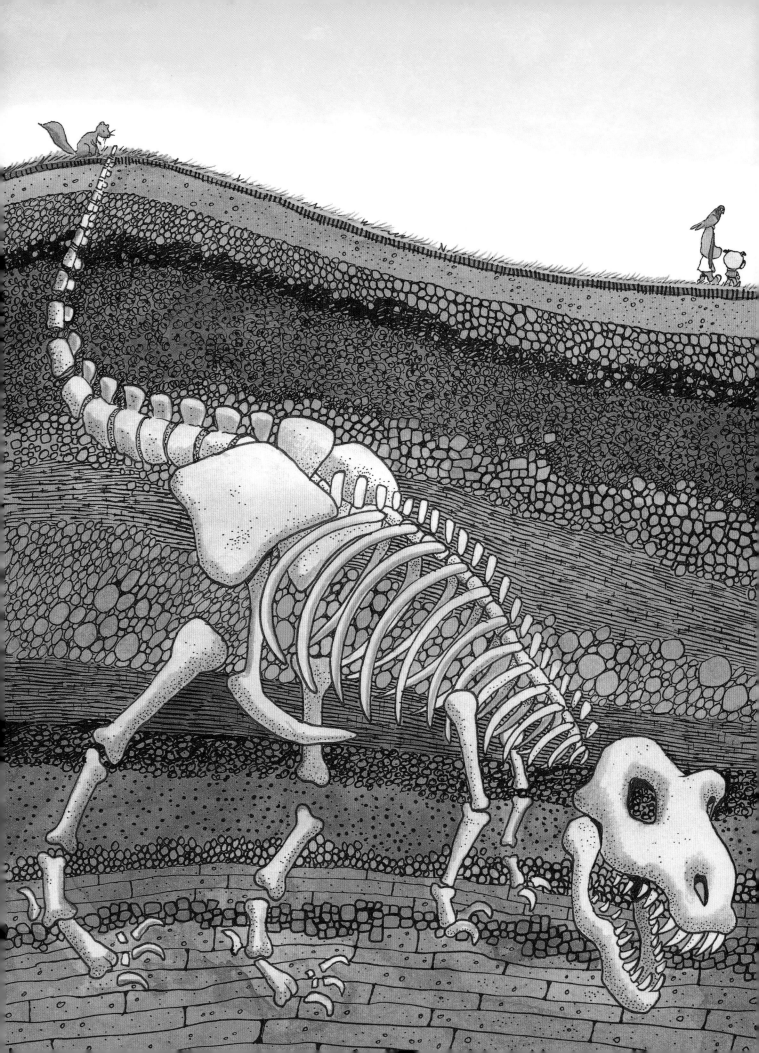

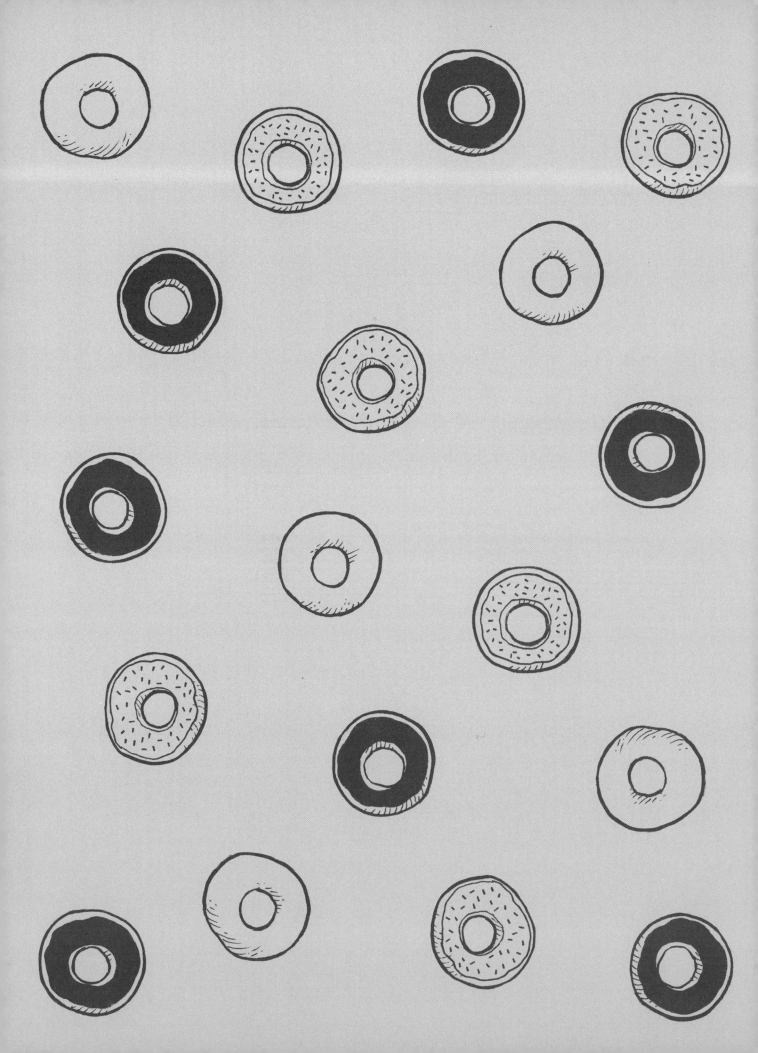